UNICORN ACADEMY
TREASURE HUNT

There was a flash of pink and the
statue exploded. Chunks of marble
flew through the air. Sunshine
whinnied and scrambled backward,
but she couldn't move fast enough.
A large stone wing was falling from
the sky toward Evie and Sunshine!

LOOK OUT FOR MORE ADVENTURES WITH

UNICORN ACADEMY

TREASURE HUNT

Lyra *and* Misty
Evie *and* Sunshine
Ivy *and* Flame
Sienna *and* Sparkle

★ ★ ★

UNICORN ACADEMY

TREASURE HUNT 2

Evie and Sunshine

JULIE SYKES
illustrated by LUCY TRUMAN

A STEPPING STONE BOOK™
Random House 🏠 New York

Text copyright © 2021 by Julie Sykes and Linda Chapman
Cover art and interior illustrations copyright © 2021 by Lucy Truman

Random House and the colophon are registered trademarks and
A Stepping Stone Book and the colophon are trademarks of
Penguin Random House LLC.

Visit us on the Web! rhcbooks.com

Educators and librarians, for a variety of teaching tools, visit us at
RHTeachersLibrarians.com

Library of Congress Cataloging-in-Publication Data
Names: Sykes, Julie, author. | Truman, Lucy, illustrator.
Title: Evie and Sunshine / Julie Sykes; illustrated by Lucy Truman.
Description: First American edition. | New York: Random House, 2023. |
Series: Unicorn Academy treasure hunt; 2 | "A Stepping Stone book." |
Audience: Ages 6–9. | Summary: Even though Evie and her unicorn, Sunshine,
may be a bit clumsy, they can still help their friends look for a hidden
treasure, but when strange accidents begin happening at the school,
they wonder if someone else is out to find the treasure too.
Identifiers: LCCN 2022039152 (print) | LCCN 2022039153 (ebook) |
ISBN 978-0-593-57145-3 (trade paperback) | ISBN 978-0-593-57147-7 (ebook)
Subjects: CYAC: Unicorns—Fiction. | Magic—Fiction. | Buried treasure—
Fiction. | Friendship—Fiction. | Boarding schools—Fiction. | Schools—Fiction.
Classification: LCC PZ7.S98325 (print) | LCC PZ7.S98325 (ebook) |
DDC [E]—dc23

Printed in the United States of America
10 9 8 7 6 5 4 3 2 1
First American Edition

For Nusaibah and Lauryn, who are super writers and know the magic of books

CHAPTER 1

"That was yummy," Evie said as she licked crumbs of chocolate cake from her fingers. The girls from Ruby dorm were having a picnic while their unicorns grazed on the lush grass. It was late spring, and the apple trees were covered with white blossoms. The bright sunlight, shining through the branches, warmed Evie's face.

"Okay," said Lyra, packing away the picnic things and double-checking that no one else was around. "Now for the important business that we came here to discuss."

"To solve the riddle on the treasure map!" said Sienna. She poked Ivy, who was lying on her back with her eyes shut. "Ivy, wake up!"

Ivy wiggled away. "I am awake. Do you have the map, Lyra?" She rolled onto her stomach.

Lyra carefully pulled two yellowed squares

of paper from her pocket. They crackled as she unfolded them and smoothed them out, placing them side by side on the picnic blanket. Each one was part of a map that had been cut into four pieces. These two each had a small picture of a crying unicorn in their outside corners. Together they made up the top half of the map. They formed a picture of Unicorn Academy and, farther down, part of a maze with half a big X in the center. The girls didn't know what the treasure at the X was, but they were determined to find out!

They had discovered the first piece hidden in a secret room above their dorm. A riddle on the back had led them to the second piece, which they had found behind an underground waterfall on the school grounds. They hoped that the riddle written on it would lead them to the third piece.

"This riddle is really annoying!" said Lyra. "What does it even mean?"

Evie pushed her wavy brown hair behind her ears. She had already memorized the riddle and recited it for the others:

"In a new folly that phantoms keep safe,
There's a space you can enter and leave with no trace.
A cold place to rest hides the circular key,
Press once and enter the d-da-dark cavity."

As Evie stumbled over the last few words, she blushed. Sometimes her mouth just couldn't seem to keep up with her brain and her words came out muddled. Luckily her friends never mentioned it, but she hated when it happened. She also tripped all the time when she was moving fast or playing sports. Evie didn't really mind not being great at sports—she liked reading more and wanted to be a scientist when she was older.

"I don't understand the first line," said Sienna.

"Phantoms are ghosts. But how can ghosts keep anywhere safe?"

"And what's 'a new folly'?" asked Ivy.

"*Folly* means foolish," said Evie.

"A new foolish that ghosts keep safe?" said Lyra. "That doesn't make any sense." She rubbed her forehead in frustration.

The word *folly* was bothering Evie too. She'd heard it before and thought it had another meaning, but she couldn't remember what.

"A cavity's a hole," said Sienna. "Could the dark cavity be the secret room where we found the first part of the map? You have to press a hidden circular button to open it up." Her eyes lit up. "Maybe that's it!"

"But the secret room isn't dark," Lyra said. "It has a window, and it's not really a cavity."

Evie reached for the map and her arm knocked against her water bottle. She hadn't screwed the

top on all the way and water splashed out. She tried to grab it, but her fingers fumbled and she sent it rolling toward the map.

"No!" cried Sienna.

Lyra picked up the map pieces before the water could reach them.

"I'm sorry!" cried Evie, jumping to her feet.

Ivy pulled some tissues out of her pocket and started to mop up the water.

"What's going on?" asked Sunshine, Evie's elegant unicorn, as she came trotting over. The other unicorns—Misty, Flame, and Sparkle—came too.

"Just Evie being clumsy again," said Sienna, grinning. "Honestly, Evie, I think we should ban you from being around food or drink. You always spill something!"

Even though Sienna was only teasing, Evie felt

awful. She tried to help by brushing the spilled water from the blanket, but, as she stepped back, she tripped over Lyra's bag and fell over.

"Oh, Evie!" groaned Sunshine. She was a very pretty unicorn with yellow, turquoise, and deep-pink patterns on her white coat that matched her long mane and tail.

"Evie, go ahead and stand by Sunshine. We'll clean up," said Ivy.

Evie went over to Sunshine and stroked her mane. She wondered if Sunshine wished she had been paired with a different student—someone who wasn't so embarrassing. Sunshine hated being the center of attention almost as much as Evie did.

How will we ever bond and graduate if Sunshine is embarrassed by me? Evie thought anxiously. During their time at Unicorn Academy, the students learned how to become guardians of Unicorn Island. They couldn't graduate until they had bonded with their unicorn and discovered their unicorn's magic power. Bonding was the highest form of friendship, and Evie would know when it happened because a lock of her hair would turn the same color as Sunshine's mane.

Lyra and Misty were the only ones in Ruby dorm to have bonded so far. Lyra now had a purple-and-green streak in her hair to prove it. Misty was also the only unicorn in Ruby dorm to have found her magic. She could form protective bubbles around people in danger. Evie couldn't wait to discover what Sunshine's magic was!

"I vote we go explore the hidden room again," said Sienna as Lyra and Ivy packed up the blanket and water bottles. "But for now let's make the most of the sun and have an obstacle race. I bet there's some stuff in that shed we could use!"

Sienna ran to a nearby garden shed and began to pull things out. The others went to help, but Sunshine stopped Evie.

"Let's just watch," she said.

Evie guessed Sunshine was worried that she would embarrass her if they tried to take part. "Okay," she said with a sigh.

The others came back with buckets, beanpoles, plant pots, hoops, and beanbags. Sienna told everyone where to put everything. When the course was set up, she climbed an apple tree with a beanbag and balanced it on a branch.

"Listen up!" she said, sliding easily back down

9

the trunk. "This is the course. First you gallop to the line of poles. You weave through them, then race to the upturned bucket where you have to reach down and pick up a plant pot. Next, ride to the pole near the apple tree, put the pot on top, then climb the apple tree to get the beanbag. Once you're back on your unicorn, jump over the fallen log and throw the beanbag through this hoop as you cross the finish line. Fastest time wins. Evie and Sunshine, you're up first."

Evie shook her head. "I'll just keep the times for everyone."

"Oh no, you have to join in. We can all take turns at timing," said Sienna.

"Yes, please join us," said Ivy.

"Pleeeease, Evie!" begged Lyra. "It'll be more fun if we all do it."

Evie hated everyone focusing on her. "Okay," she said, giving in, even though she could feel a

knot of anxiety tightening in her chest. She saw Sunshine give her a worried look.

"Evie, I don't think this is a good idea," said Sunshine in a low voice as Evie got onto her back.

Evie swallowed. "I promise I'll try not to embarrass you," she murmured.

"It's not that. It's—"

"Come on, they're waiting for us to start," interrupted Evie.

Lyra had the stopwatch. "Three, two, one, go!" she shouted.

Sunshine set off. Evie gripped her mane as they cantered to the poles. Sunshine weaved gracefully between them, and Evie could hear the others cheering them on.

So far so good, she thought as Sunshine galloped to the bucket and pole by the apple tree. Leaning down, she picked up the plant pot from the upturned bucket. *Don't drop it, don't drop it,* she told herself. To her relief Sunshine stood absolutely still while she slipped it on top of the pole. *Phew! Now for the tree!*

"Please be *very* careful," Sunshine begged her as Evie dismounted and ran over to it, moving carefully around daffodils at the base of the trunk. Gritting her teeth, Evie pulled herself up until she reached the branch where the beanbag was balanced. Keeping one arm wrapped around the tree trunk, Evie stretched out to grab it.

Beneath her, Sunshine pawed at the ground anxiously.

"Be careful, Evie!" she whinnied.

With a shriek, Evie lost her balance and hung

underneath the branch, clinging on with her hands and feet. She heard a faint popping noise, and suddenly the tree shook violently as if it had just been hit. Evie gasped as her grip on the trunk loosened and she fell. . . .

CHAPTER 2

"Evie!" her friends yelled.

Sunshine whinnied and leaped forward to try to catch her, but Misty was already stamping her hoof and using her magic. A large, shimmering bubble formed around Evie and carried her gently to the ground, where it came to a stop before popping. Evie sat on the grass, her heart pounding. If Misty hadn't used her magic, she could have been really hurt.

"Are you okay?" Lyra, Ivy, and Sienna cried, galloping over on their unicorns.

"I'm fine!" said Evie, knowing her face was

as red as a tomato. She looked at the daffodils she had crushed when she landed. "I don't know what happened." She was sure she'd felt the tree shake when she'd been hanging on, but maybe she'd imagined it. She'd probably just been dizzy because she'd been upside down. "Thanks, Misty."

"No problem," said Misty.

Sunshine seemed scared and embarrassed as she nuzzled her. "I'm really glad you're not hurt."

Lyra helped Evie to her feet. "Do you want to finish the course?" she asked.

Evie shook her head. "I think I'll head inside," she said, pulling a twig from her hair.

"I'll come with you," Ivy offered.

"It's okay. I'll be fine." Evie's eyes stung. Why couldn't she just be like everyone else? Her foot throbbed as she hobbled back to Sunshine. They walked to the stables in silence.

When they entered her stall, Sunshine finally spoke. "Next time there's an obstacle race or something like that, I think we should just watch, Evie."

"Okay," Evie muttered. She didn't want to embarrass Sunshine.

After filling up Sunshine's hay net and fluffing up her straw bed, Evie left the stables. As she walked toward the school buildings, she started to feel better. It was hard to be miserable when Unicorn Academy was so beautiful. The gardens were bursting with spring flowers, and the glass-and-marble towers of the school sparkled against the clear blue sky. Evie's chest filled with pride. *I might not be good at sports, but I'm a good student and I'm great at science and math,* she reminded herself as she went inside. *There's no reason I can't be an excellent guardian of Unicorn Island.*

Sam, one of the boys from Topaz dorm, was

coming down the hall, pulling a suitcase on wheels. A lady with dark, shoulder-length hair and lots of jewelry was walking beside him, pulling a much larger case. Evie recognized her as Dr. Angelica Briar, Sam's aunt and a famous archaeologist. She'd visited the academy earlier in the year to give a talk on her work, and Ruby dorm had shown her the first piece of the map. Dr. Briar had told them it was about a hundred years old, but that it wasn't worth anything.

Sam whispered something to his aunt and then greeted Evie. "Hi there!"

"Hi, Sam," Evie said. "Hello, Dr. Briar."

Dr. Briar smiled warmly. "Evie, isn't it? You were one of the girls who found that old piece of paper, weren't you?"

Evie was excited that Dr. Briar had remembered her. "Yes, that's right."

"Aunt Angelica is staying for a few weeks to help document the paintings and artifacts in the school," said Sam proudly.

"So, have you and your friends found any other bits of old paper that you want me to take a look at?" Dr. Briar's eyes twinkled.

Evie only just stopped herself from saying that they had found a second piece. She'd have liked to tell Dr. Briar, but Lyra had made them promise to keep the map secret.

"Well?" pressed Dr. Briar, her eyes curious.

"No." A blush crept up Evie's cheeks as she lied. To hide her discomfort, she blurted out a question. "Dr. Briar, do you know what *folly* means?" She'd been pondering that ever since she'd been in the orchard.

"Why, yes I do," said Dr. Briar. "It means foolish, but it's also the name given to a structure that's built for fun and has no useful purpose. Many years ago rich people liked to build follies on their property. They could be towers or even miniature castles."

Of course! Evie suddenly remembered reading about a secret folly in a book. Her eyes widened. Maybe the new folly in the riddle was a building—a place that had recently been built when the map was drawn.

"Why do you ask?" Dr. Briar asked, studying her.

"Oh, n-no reason," Evie stammered. "I just

heard the word somewhere and didn't know what it meant." Evie felt uncomfortable under Dr. Briar's gaze. "Well, I'd better go," she said. "Nice to see you, Dr. Briar. Bye, Sam!"

She didn't stop until she was in Ruby dorm at the top of the north tower. She sank down on her bed, impatient for the others to come back so she could tell them what she'd discovered!

CHAPTER 3

A little while later, Lyra and Sienna came running up the stairs with Ivy following more slowly.

"I won!" Sienna announced gleefully. "Ivy couldn't get the beanbag through the hoop, and Lyra and Misty knocked a pole over."

Ivy flopped down on her bed. "I'm exhausted!"

"Is your foot okay?" Lyra asked Evie. "You looked like you were limping earlier."

Evie could hardly contain her excitement. "It's fine now. But I have something to tell you all! I saw Dr. Briar earlier, and—"

"Dr. Briar!" Lyra broke in. "Why is she back

here? I know she's Sam's aunt, but I don't trust her."

"Me either," Sienna added. "Remember when we showed her the first piece of the map and she looked like she wasn't going to give it back?"

"Yes, and—"

"Shush, you two!" interrupted Ivy. "Evie said she has something to tell us. Go on, Evie."

Evie gave Ivy a grateful look. It was sometimes hard to get a word in when Sienna and Lyra got talking. She took a breath. "Dr. Briar is here to document the paintings and stuff. I asked her if she knew what a folly was, and she told me it's a building, like a tower, built just for fun."

"So there could be a folly here on the academy grounds?" said Lyra, her green eyes lighting up.

Evie nodded. "Or the riddle could mean somewhere else on the island."

"A folly guarded by ghosts," breathed Sienna.

They all looked at each other in excitement.

"This might be what we need to solve the riddle!" said Lyra. "You're a star, Evie!"

"Yes, you're absolutely amazing!" declared Sienna.

Evie glowed in delight.

Sienna grabbed Lyra's shoulder. "We're going to find the treasure map," she chanted.

"We're going to find the treasure!" Lyra sang back.

The door, which the girls had left ajar, opened, and Nawaz, Archie, and Reuben from Topaz dorm looked in.

"What are you all shouting about?" asked Nawaz.

"Nothing!" Lyra said quickly.

Sam appeared behind the other boys. "What's going on?"

"The girls have gone loopy," said Reuben. "They were shouting about finding treasure."

Sam's face stiffened. "Treasure?"

"Lyra and Sienna were just messing around," said Ivy.

"Hey, we were hoping to catch you," said Sienna. "We wanted to challenge you to a cross-net match tomorrow."

Evie smiled to herself—Sienna was so quick at making things up. It was the first she'd heard about a crossnet match.

"Ruby versus Topaz," added Lyra.

"Cool," said Archie.

They discussed the details and agreed to meet at the crossnet field at ten the next morning. But as the boys left, Evie saw Sam give the girls a look just like the one Dr. Briar had given her in the hall earlier.

"Whoops, that was close!" whispered Sienna as Lyra shut the door.

Lyra made a face. "I can't believe we shouted about treasure. Did you see the way Sam was looking at us as he left? I hope he doesn't suspect anything. Remember when someone ransacked our dorm just after we found the first piece? We thought it was a prank, but what if Dr. Briar was lying when she said that the map wasn't valuable? What if she or Sam searched our dorm trying to find it?" She patted her pockets. "From now on, these are never leaving my sight—we're not letting anyone else find the treasure!"

★

Evie couldn't sleep that night. She kept thinking about the crossnet match. Crossnet was played with teams of two or four, and the idea was to ride up and down the field, throwing the ball using sticks with nets on the end. Goals were scored when the ball was put through the opposing team's hoop. Evie always ended up dropping the ball. It was fine playing with her friends, who never seemed to care, but it would be really embarrassing to mess up in front of Topaz dorm.

She got up at sunrise and went to the window. She could see right across the grounds. Beyond Sparkle Lake were the meadows, and past them were the woods where they'd found the cave and the second piece of the map. On the other side of the woods was a smaller grove of trees. One tree in the middle looked taller than the rest. Evie blinked. Was it a tree, or could it be the top of a tower? It was hard to tell. She glanced around at her sleeping friends. Should she mention it

to them? But if she did, Lyra would want to go there, and if Evie was wrong and it was just a tall tree, she'd feel embarrassed. *Maybe I should do some research first,* she thought. *I could go to the library instead of playing crossnet.*

By the time the rest of Ruby dorm woke up, Evie had decided.

"I'm not going to play in the crossnet match," she told them. "I'm going to the library instead to see if I can find out if there are any follies on the school grounds."

"But if you don't play, we won't be able to have teams of four," said Sienna.

"You can play in pairs and add the points up over several rounds," Evie suggested. "Or play in teams of three. That way one person can act as a referee."

Lyra frowned. "This isn't because of what happened in the obstacle race yesterday, is it?"

Evie rubbed her nose. "It is, kind of." *And it'll make Sunshine happier if I don't play and embarrass her,* she added to herself.

Ivy put her arm through Evie's. "We'd rather lose and have you as part of the team than win without you."

"Absolutely," said Lyra.

Evie saw Sienna hesitate, but then she nodded. "Of course we'd rather you played," she said.

Evie knew Sienna was being nice. Her friend didn't like losing any competition. But she was grateful Sienna cared about her feelings enough to lie. "I really want to do some research. You play without me."

Although Lyra and Ivy continued trying to change her mind, Evie stood her ground. When the others went to get their unicorns ready, she went with them to explain to Sunshine that she wasn't playing in the match.

"Good. I think it's for the best," Sunshine said, looking relieved.

Evie felt a flicker of disappointment. A small part of her had hoped Sunshine would say that it didn't matter if she messed up, that her friends really wanted her to join. She sighed. "I guess so."

"You do *want* to miss the match, don't you, Evie?" said Sunshine, giving her a concerned look.

"Yes. No. I mean, I know it's for the best," said Evie. She saw that Sunshine was watching her, worried. "I'll get you some sky berries, and then I'm going to the library."

Evie was coming back from the storeroom with a bucket of sky berries—the unicorns' favorite food—when there was a loud bang from Sunshine's stall. Evie ran to the door.

Sunshine stood in the entrance. She was cov-

ered in hay. It hung from her nose like a droopy mustache and stuck to her legs, making her look like a shaggy pony. A giggle rose in Evie's throat, but Sunshine looked so shocked that she bit it back. "What's going on?"

"Um . . . I stamped my hoof, and my—my hay net burst," stammered Sunshine.

Evie squeezed past her unicorn, her eyes widening as she took in the mess. "Are you sure you're okay? How did it happen?"

"It must have been the way you tied it up. It fell down and exploded," said Sunshine.

Evie felt shame rush through her. She *had* filled it very full, but she thought she'd tied it up correctly. "Oh gosh. I'm so sorry! I'll refill it and sweep up."

"Don't worry. I can eat the hay from the floor," said Sunshine. "You can go to the library," she added quickly. "Really, it's fine!"

Evie swallowed. "Okay, well, see you later, then." Feeling unhappy, she headed back to school. Unicorns and their partners were supposed to want to be together. If Sunshine wouldn't even let her clean up her stall, she must really be wishing that she'd been paired with someone else!

★

Evie went straight to the library and found a box of old maps in the reference section. She took one of the school grounds and carefully spread it out on a nearby table. The map smelled musty, and the ink was beginning to fade. Evie studied it closely. On the western side of the woods, she saw the cave that had led to the underground river. Beyond that there was a smaller grove of trees. The middle was marked with a triangle. She squinted at the old-fashioned writing next to it and read *folly*. Excitement leaped through her.

"Do you need any help?" Ms. Tansy, the librarian, asked.

Evie looked up eagerly. "Do you know anything about this folly?"

Ms. Tansy looked at the map through her yellow-rimmed, flower-shaped glasses. "I don't, but there's a book about follies of the island. It might be mentioned in there." She hurried off and returned with a thick book open in her hands. "Here you go," she said. *"The folly at the academy, built to look like an ancient tower, was constructed about a hundred years ago in the middle of Spiny Grove."*

A hundred years ago. Evie's brain whirred. Dr. Briar had told them she thought the first piece of the map was about a hundred years old. Was that just a coincidence, or could this be the new folly mentioned in the clue, a folly built at the same time the map was made?

"Apparently there were all sorts of stories about it being haunted. After several students claimed they saw and heard ghosts near it, it was abandoned. There's a picture here—of the tower, not the ghosts!" Ms. Tansy chuckled.

Evie stared at the black-and-white photo that showed a round stone building topped with a

cone-shaped roof. An idea grew in her mind as she remembered a line from the riddle: *In a new folly that phantoms keep safe*. Was the tower really haunted, or had someone started that rumor to keep people away after hiding part of the treasure map there?

Evie asked if she could borrow the book, and Ms. Tansy carried it over to her desk and checked it out. As she passed it back to Evie, Dr. Briar arrived.

"Hello, Evie."

"Hello," said Evie. Her fingers fumbled with the book and it thudded to the floor.

"Allow me." Dr. Briar picked the book up and

glanced at the title. "Follies," she said, raising her eyebrows. "You were asking me about follies yesterday, weren't you?"

Evie nodded.

"Are you interested in them?" Dr. Briar asked.

"Evie is one of our brightest students," said Ms. Tansy. "She's interested in everything. We were just talking about the folly on the school grounds. Maybe you know something about it, Dr. Briar? Apparently it's haunted!"

Dr. Briar smiled. "I suppose so, if you believe in ghosts. Although there have been many sightings, so maybe there is truth in the stories after all!" She turned to Evie. "Why are you so curious about the school folly? That wasn't where you and your friends found that old piece of paper you showed me, was it?"

"No," said Evie, glad to be telling the truth. "It wasn't."

"I'd be very careful if you're planning a trip there," said Dr. Briar, studying her closely. "The building is very old, and it may be dangerous."

Evie felt a blush rise in her cheeks. "Thanks!"

Dr. Briar studied her as if she was an artifact under a microscope.

Evie got redder and redder.

Ms. Tansy looked from one to the other. "Well, run along now, Evie dear," she said brightly, breaking the silence.

Dr. Briar handed Evie the book. "Yes, off you go," she said.

Evie hurried out of the library in relief. But as she reached the door, she glanced back and saw Dr. Briar watching her leave.

CHAPTER 4

Evie settled down in the dorm and read, her eyes quickly skimming over the words. The folly on the grounds had been built a hundred years ago by a head teacher called Ms. Evergreen. According to the book, Ms. Evergreen had been a fascinating woman, a brave and passionate guardian of the island. Before becoming head teacher, she had been an archaeologist and had spent many years searching for a precious jewel known as the Unicorn's Diamond.

"The Unicorn's Diamond," Evie whispered aloud, feeling a shiver of excitement. The dia-

mond was legendary for both its beauty and its power.

Just then her friends came up the stairs, talking loudly.

Sienna threw the door open. "We won. We beat the boys five matches to three."

"It was fun, and when we got back to the stables, there was an explosion!" added Lyra. "One of the automated trolleys was moving along with a bucket full of sky berries. It was just passing Sunshine's stall when there was a loud bang. The berries exploded and went everywhere."

"Really?" Evie's eyes widened. "Was anyone hurt?"

Ivy grinned. "No, but there was a huge mess. We had to wash Sunshine's mane. It turned blue with sky-berry juice. "

"Is she okay?"

"She's fine," said Ivy, putting a comforting arm

39

around Evie. "Ms. Tulip thought the berries may have exploded because they were from last season and they'd been left in a warm cupboard. Sunshine seemed a bit shocked at first, but we cleaned her up and left her munching on some hay. She said not to tell you, but we thought you'd want to know."

Evie wondered why Sunshine hadn't wanted her to come and help, but she pushed the thought away as she remembered her news. "You'll never guess what I've found out," she said.

They all sat on her bed while Evie explained what she'd discovered about the folly on the grounds.

"Ms. Evergreen, who built it, was head teacher here a hundred years ago. She sounds awesome. She had been an archaeologist before, and she'd spent years searching for the Unicorn's Diamond."

"The Unicorn's Diamond," said Lyra. "A beautiful diamond that grants the heart's desire of anyone who holds it. Isn't that just a legend?"

"This book says no one knows for sure," said Evie. She glanced at its pages. "The legend says it was created in ancient times, formed from the tears of joy shed by Unicorn Island's original unicorn, Daybreak, on the birth of her first foal. The—"

"Daybreak?" interrupted Sienna. "Hang on! Isn't that the unicorn on the tapestry downstairs that hides the entrance to the secret room?"

"Yes, and we had to follow carvings of Daybreak to get to the second piece of the map," said Ivy.

Evie gasped.

"What is it?" demanded Lyra.

"Have . . . have you got th-the map?" Evie asked, stumbling over her words in her excitement.

"Yes. Why?" Lyra pulled the pieces out of her pocket and placed them on the bed.

"Look!" Evie exclaimed as she pointed to the top corner of each piece. "There are pictures of Daybreak here too, in each corner. Could the map take you to—"

"The Unicorn's Diamond!" finished Lyra.

They all stared at each other.

"Do you really think this map could lead us to the diamond?" whispered Sienna.

"Yes! I do!" Evie picked up her book again and read a paragraph out loud. *"According to the legend, anyone who holds the diamond in their hand will be granted their heart's desire. For centuries people have wanted the diamond in order to ask for their greatest wish. But the diamond, if it ever existed, has been so well hidden that so far no one has found it."* She looked up, her eyes shining. "But maybe Ms. Evergreen did find it—"

Lyra broke in. "And hid it somewhere safe so that people couldn't get their hands on it. It would be awful if it was found by someone who wanted to make bad things happen."

Evie nodded. "But Ms. Evergreen made a map so that it could be found again if it needed to be.

She cut it into four pieces and hid them on the school grounds."

"And if we find the rest of the map, we'll find the diamond!" said Lyra, looking as if she was about to burst with excitement.

"We have to find it," said Sienna.

Lyra jumped up. "Let's go find the folly right now!"

"We can't," said Ivy. "It's lunchtime."

"After lunch, then," said Lyra.

"Wait. Spiny Grove, where the folly is, is at the edge of the school grounds," said Evie. "We won't be able to get there and back before dark. We'll have to wait until Saturday."

Sienna nodded. "We could tell Ms. Rivers we want to look at the wildlife and ask if we can take a picnic with us. Then we can have the whole day to explore the tower."

There was a faint noise outside their dorm door.

Lyra hurried over and pulled the door open, but there was no one there.

She shut it behind her again. "Phew! I thought for a moment someone was listening to us. This has to be our secret. We can't tell anyone about it. Promise?"

They all nodded. "Promise!"

CHAPTER 5

At breakfast the next morning, Evie was surprised when Dr. Briar called her over to where she was sitting with Ms. Nettles.

"Evie, I wonder if I could ask you for a favor." The jeweled rings on Dr. Briar's fingers flashed as she patted a strand of her dark hair into place. "The academy has more works of art than I realized. Would you like to help me today?"

"Me?" Evie was confused. Had Dr. Briar really meant to ask her, or had she meant Lyra, who

everyone knew wanted to be an archaeologist when she was older?

But no, Dr. Briar was looking right at her and smiling encouragingly.

Evie's cheeks heated up. It was nice to be singled out in such a way. "Yes, please," she said immediately.

"Perfect. Meet me in the hall at lunchtime, and I'll show you what needs to be done."

Evie almost floated out of the dining hall, but Lyra frowned when Evie told them about the conversation. "She asked you to help? Why? Sam knows how much I love archaeology." Her frown deepened. "Make sure you don't tell them anything about the map."

"Of course she won't say anything," said Ivy.

Evie was hurt that Lyra felt like she needed to remind her. While the others got ready for their

first class, she went to the stables to talk to Sunshine about it.

As she approached Sunshine's stall, Evie heard a bang and saw a pink spark shoot out of the doorway. Evie rushed forward, her heart in her mouth. "Sunshine!" she cried. "Was that you? Have you found your magic?"

Sunshine popped her head out of her stall.

"No!" she said quickly. "I haven't. Definitely not! Why are you here, Evie?"

Her voice was almost unfriendly. Evie stopped in her tracks. She thought she'd seen a spark of magic. "I . . . I just wanted to talk to you about something."

"Can it wait?" said Sunshine. It seemed like she didn't want Evie to go into her stall.

"Yes, I guess," said Evie. Sunshine had never spoken to her like that before. "I'll, um, come back later."

"I'll see you at break, then," said Sunshine.

Evie turned away. What was up with Sunshine? She was acting as though Evie had really upset her. Feeling confused, Evie headed back to school.

★

Evie didn't visit Sunshine at break. She didn't want to risk her unicorn being unfriendly to her in front of everyone. At lunchtime she waited for

Dr. Briar in the hall. In the center of the room was the magic map, which showed all of Unicorn Island. It could transport people and their unicorns anywhere on the island, but there was a magical force field protecting it, and students were only allowed to use it with a teacher's permission.

The walls of the hall were covered with huge paintings of famous unicorns and previous head teachers. When Dr. Briar arrived with Sam, she asked Sam and Evie to work their way around the room and write down the title and artist of each painting, along with some brief notes.

Evie felt shy at first. Sam always seemed a little stuck-up, but right now he was much more friendly. He knew lots of interesting stories about the artists who had painted the pictures.

"How do you know so much?" she asked.

"My mom's an art historian," Sam replied. "She's taught me lots about art. I spend time with Aunt Angelica during the holidays too." He nodded toward Dr. Briar, who was studying a large pink vase. "I've helped her on tons of digs." He smiled at Evie. "I don't know nearly as much as you do about science and math, though. You're really smart."

Evie felt a warm glow. "Thanks," she muttered, thinking how much nicer Sam was when he was on his own.

Sam's aunt called him over and had a quiet conversation with him. When he returned, he looked uncomfortable. "So," he said, "what have you and the rest of your dorm been up to? You always seem to be whispering about something. What's the big secret?"

Evie was surprised at the change of subject.

"Nothing," she said. "There's no big secret. Who's this painting by?" she asked, moving on to a portrait of an old head teacher.

"Finoula Sparrow," said Sam, following her. "Did you know there are supposed to be lots of secret passages and hidden rooms in the academy? I'd love to find one, wouldn't you?" He looked at her intently.

"I guess," said Evie uneasily.

"But you haven't found any secret places yet?" asked Sam.

"No, definitely not," said Evie quickly. She turned away. "I'm going to make some notes on the statues over there."

As she walked away from Sam, she glanced at Dr. Briar, who was giving Sam a questioning look.

He shook his head. Evie frowned, suddenly certain that Dr. Briar and Sam were up to something. Why had Dr. Briar asked her to help and not Lyra? Did she think that Evie would tell her what they were up to?

Well, they can try all they like, but they're not going to get any information about the map out of me, she thought.

She stopped by the statues and wrote down some notes. She was sure Dr. Briar and Sam were both still watching her.

★

After lunch, in Geography and Culture class, Ms. Rivers announced that they were going on a scavenger hunt on the school grounds with their unicorns.

"I'll give you a list of artifacts to find," Ms. Rivers told them. "Answer the questions about them, and the first team to return with the correct answers will win a prize."

"This is the best lesson ever!" said Sienna as they got their unicorns.

The boys from Topaz dorm were ready first. "We are so going to win! Watch us and weep, Ruby dorm!" Sam cried, before galloping away with his friends.

"I don't know how you spent all lunchtime with him," Sienna said to Evie, making a face.

"It was a little weird," said Evie. She wondered if she should mention her suspicions about Sam and Dr. Briar, but she didn't have any proof. She decided to keep quiet for now.

To Evie's relief, Sunshine seemed back to her usual friendly self that afternoon. "This is fun!" she whinnied as they galloped toward the rose gardens with the others.

The girls visited the rose gardens, the Safari Trail, the playground, the vegetable garden, and

the lake, ticking nine of the ten items off their list. "We just need a winged unicorn statue now," said Lyra.

"There's one in the orchard," said Evie.

As they approached the orchard, Topaz dorm appeared at a gallop from the direction of the playground. "Faster! They're going to the orchard too," Sienna shouted.

Ruby dorm raced into the orchard with the boys right behind them. The rearing unicorn with wings was by a pear tree. Sunshine reached the statue first, the rest of Rudy dorm close behind. She stopped suddenly in front of it, making Evie slip sideways on her back. Evie steadied herself, holding tightly on to Sunshine's mane. "Are you okay, Evie?" Sunshine asked, anxiously stamping her feet.

"Yes, yes, I'm—"

But Evie broke off as there was a flash of pink and the statue exploded.

Chunks of marble flew through the air. Sunshine whinnied and scrambled backward, but she couldn't move fast enough. A large stone wing was falling from the sky toward them!

CHAPTER 6

Evie was sure the wing was going to hit them, but, at the last moment, time seemed to stop. The wing froze in the air above their heads. Sunshine reared backward, and then time restarted.

Whumph! The marble wing thumped onto the ground exactly where Evie and Sunshine had been a few seconds ago.

"Evie! Sunshine! Are you okay?" cried Lyra.

"What happened?" gasped Evie. "I thought it was going to hit us, but it just stopped in midair!"

"It was Flash!" Sam burst out, jumping off and hugging his unicorn. "I saw sparks fly from his

hooves and I smelled burnt sugar. He must have gotten his magic—pausing magic! It means he can make things stop for a few seconds."

"Oh wow!" said Evie. "That's awesome magic. You saved our lives, Flash. Thank you so much. You're amazing!"

Flash, a tall unicorn with a silver-and-green mane, looked very proud as everyone crowded around, congratulating him and Sam.

"Now that you've found your magic, we just

need to bond. Then we'll be able to graduate at the end of the year," said Sam, smiling and giving Flash another hug.

"But why did the statue explode in the first place?" asked Lyra, frowning as she looked at the chunks of marble lying on the grass all around them.

"You didn't bump into it, did you?" Sienna asked Evie.

"No!" Evie said.

"It's really weird," said Lyra, riding around the base of the statue. "Statues shouldn't just explode for no reason. I guess we'd better tell Ms. Rivers."

"We'll tell her," said Sam. "We're the fastest dorm. Come on, guys!" He hopped back onto Flash, and he and the other boys raced off.

Sienna scowled. "Sam can be so annoying."

"He did help save me and Sunshine, though," said Evie. "I wonder why that statue exploded."

"Evie, can we go back to the stables now?" Sunshine said. "I'm feeling a bit shaky."

"Of course," said Evie, patting her. She turned to the others. "You know, there have been quite a few explosions recently."

"What do you mean?" asked Ivy.

"Well, the sky berries exploded when you were at the stables, and Sunshine's hay net burst the day before. I thought it was my fault, that I had stuffed it too full and hadn't tied it up correctly, but—"

"Evie, I really do want to go back," interrupted Sunshine. "I'm not feeling well."

"Okay," said Evie. "I'd better go," she told the others.

"We'll come with you," said Lyra, riding up

alongside them. "The boys have won the scavenger hunt now anyway. So you think someone might be making things explode around us on purpose?"

"Maybe it's someone who knows we've found part of the map," said Sienna. "And they want to scare us."

"Or hurt us," said Ivy with a shiver.

"But the only people who know we have a piece of the map are Dr. Briar and Sam," said Evie.

Lyra looked thoughtful. "The statue exploded just as Sam reached it, and he was there that day in the stables when the sky berries exploded." Her mouth tightened. "I bet Dr. Briar is getting him to scare us because she knows we've found part of the map and wants it for herself. I knew she was interested in it, even though she pretended it was worthless!"

"But Sam can't be making things explode. Flash has pausing magic, not exploding magic," Evie pointed out.

"True, but maybe there's a spell or potion that can cause explosions," said Lyra. "Well, Sam and Dr. Briar had better watch out. They're not going to stop us from finding the next part of the map. We're going to search the folly on Saturday, and then the third piece will be ours!"

★

On Saturday the girls woke early. They had permission from Ms. Rivers to go on a picnic ride, so they went to the dining hall to get their packed lunches. On the table next to their lunches, there was also a packed lunch with Dr. Briar's name on it.

Lyra frowned. "Why does Dr. Briar need a packed lunch?"

"Who cares," said Sienna. "Let's get going."

They grabbed some fresh croissants to eat on the way and set off.

It was another gorgeous day. Sparkle Lake glittered in the bright sunshine and the birds were singing. The unicorns cantered through the meadows and paused at the stream to get a drink. They rode on through the beautiful academy grounds, but as they got closer to Spiny Grove, the birds stopped singing and it got darker. The

tall trees were clustered closely together as if they wanted to keep people out. Vines wound around their trunks. The girls paused at the start of the path, no one wanting to be the first to go in.

Ivy shivered. "What if the folly really is haunted?"

"It's not," said Lyra. "There are no such things as ghosts."

"You hope!" Sienna said.

Evie thought back to what Ms. Tansy had said about some students thinking they'd seen ghosts near the folly. She hoped it was a rumor encouraged by Ms. Evergreen to keep people away!

Lyra rode into the trees, and Sienna and Ivy followed. To Evie's surprise, Sunshine hung back.

"Come on," she said. "We don't want to get left behind."

Sunshine cantered after the others, but Evie could feel her trembling. She frowned. Sunshine

wasn't usually shy when it came to adventures, so what was bothering her?

The path was narrow and gloomy, the trees blocking out the light. It was quiet, and the air was cold. As the unicorns pushed their way along the overgrown path, the branches tugged at their legs and tails, and the shadows grew darker.

"I really don't like it here," said Ivy nervously.

"Neither do I," said Sunshine to Evie. "It's so dark."

A spooky "WHOOOO-OOOO" rang through the air, and a pale shape glimmered for a moment, high in the trees, before disappearing.

Ivy shrieked, and Evie grabbed a handful of mane as Sunshine jumped.

Sienna gasped. "Was that a ghost?"

"It can't be," said Lyra. She stroked Misty, who was trembling. "Ghosts aren't real."

"I really don't like this, Evie," said Sunshine, her voice shaking.

Evie took a deep breath to calm her racing heart. "Don't worry, I'm sure we'll be okay," she reassured her. "Lyra's right. Ghosts aren't real."

"It's not the ghosts. It's the . . ." Sunshine's voice trailed off. "It doesn't matter," she muttered.

"We have to keep going," said Lyra, urging Misty forward. "Look, there's something over there, through the trees!"

Evie caught a glimpse of golden stone in the distance. "I bet it's the folly. Come on, Sunshine, we're almost there!"

They all rode on. As the path widened, Evie saw a tall tower made of yellow stone in a clearing ahead. Its crumbling walls looked like they were being held together by the dark-green ivy

that covered them. There was
an old wooden door and
a stone bench outside it.
Excitement bubbled up
inside Evie, squashing
her fears. This could be
it! They could be about
to find the third piece of
the map!

Sunshine paused by the bench. "Oh wow,"
breathed Evie, dismounting and walking toward
the tower.

"This is so exciting!" said Lyra as Misty stopped
beside Sunshine and she jumped off too. "I hope
we find the—"

Then she gasped as the door opened and Dr.
Briar walked out!

CHAPTER 7

"Hello, girls." Dr. Briar smiled brightly as a tall, slim unicorn came out of the tower beside her. "Ms. Nettles mentioned you were going out for a picnic ride today. I hope you weren't planning on exploring this folly?"

The girls gaped at her. Even Lyra seemed lost for words.

Dr. Briar sighed. "It is a very interesting building, but I'm afraid you can't come inside. My research suggests that a previous head teacher may have hidden a special artifact here. Ms. Nettles has given me permission to conduct a

search. The tower and these woods are now off-limits to all students until I have completed my work. I'm sure you understand." She continued to smile, but Evie saw a hint of triumph in her eyes.

"How did you get here so fast?" said Lyra, finding her voice at last. "You were still at school when we left."

"Solomon and I used the magic map," said Dr. Briar, patting her unicorn. "It makes traveling between here and the school so much easier. It's a shame students aren't allowed to use it. Now, off you go. I'm sure you can find another place to have your little"—she paused—"*picnic.*"

Evie couldn't bear the thought of Dr. Briar finding the next clue before them, but there was nothing they could do about it. She walked over

to Sunshine, but on the way her foot snagged on a tree root, sending her sprawling.

"Are you okay?" Ivy called.

"I'm fine." Evie pulled herself up, but as she did so, her eyes fell on a small round indentation under one arm of the bench. The circle contained a tiny picture of a crying unicorn. Evie gasped. It looked exactly like the button that opened the staircase to the hidden room where they had found the first part of the map.

A line from the clue jumped into her head: *A cold place to rest hides the circular key.* Could this be it? The way to find the third piece? After all, the bench was definitely a cold place to rest.

"Evie?" said Lyra in concern. "Are you hurt?"

"N-no," Evie stammered, getting to her feet. She could feel Dr. Briar watching them and didn't want to say anything in front of her. "I'm fine. Let's go." She got back on Sunshine, and the girls left.

"I can't believe Dr. Briar is searching the folly!" Lyra said when they were out of earshot.

"It's so not fair!" said Sienna.

"Dr. Briar's going to find the next piece of the map before us now," groaned Ivy.

"Maybe not," said Evie, her eyes shining.

They all looked at her. "What do you mean?" asked Lyra.

"I'll tell you when we're somewhere private," said Evie, glancing around at the trees. There was no way of knowing who or what was hiding in them. "Come on!"

Only when they reached a meadow far away from the grove did Evie ask Sunshine to stop.

She slid off, and the others joined her as she sat down on the grass. "I saw something," she said. Even though they were on their own, she kept her voice low as she told them about the button she'd spotted under the bench.

"Think of the other two pieces of the map," Evie said eagerly. "They were really well hidden. There's no way Ms. Evergreen would have just left the third piece lying around in the tower. She's bound to have put it in a good hiding place. I think the button is important. Remember the riddle. It says:

In a new folly that phantoms keep safe,

There's a space you can enter and leave with no trace.

A cold place to rest hides the circular key,

Press once and enter the dark cavity."

She looked at her friends. "I think the button is the circular key, and the map's hiding place—*the dark cavity*—will be revealed if we press it!"

"I bet you're right!" Lyra cried.

"So Dr. Briar won't find the map unless she finds that button," said Sienna, smiling. "But because she hasn't seen the second piece, she won't even know to look for it!"

"We can still beat her!" exclaimed Ivy.

"How are we going to get to the tower without her seeing?" asked Evie. She sighed. "I guess we just have to wait until she abandons her search."

Lyra grinned. "Or we go to the tower when she's not there—at night!"

"No way!" Ivy squeaked.

"I'm with Ivy. Those woods are scary enough in the daytime," agreed Sienna.

"You want to find the map, don't you?" Lyra said.

They nodded.

"Then stop worrying about ghosts and get ready for a midnight adventure!" she declared.

CHAPTER 8

"What I don't understand is how Dr. Briar knew to search in the folly," said Sienna as they got into their beds that night. They had decided to get some sleep before setting off at midnight when everyone else in the school would be in bed.

"I don't know," said Lyra, pulling her red-spotted blanket up to her chin. "You didn't say anything when you were helping her, did you, Evie?"

"Evie wouldn't," said Ivy loyally.

Evie felt uncomfortable. "I didn't say anything, but it might have been my fault that she guessed about the folly." Her friends looked at her as she confessed. "I bumped into Dr. Briar that time I went to the library, and she saw me checking out the book on follies. She must have realized I was interested in the school folly. I'm really sorry I wasn't more careful." She glanced up, wondering if the others were going to be upset with her, but they all just shrugged.

"It's not your fault. There's no way you could have known Dr. Briar was going to be in the library," said Ivy. "Or that she'd realize why you had a book on follies."

"And if you hadn't borrowed that book, we might never have known about the folly ourselves," Sienna pointed out.

"I'm glad you went to the library that day," said Lyra.

Evie felt a rush of relief.

"If it's anyone's fault, it's mine and Sienna's,"

Lyra went on. "We were the ones who were shouting about treasure. I bet Sam told Dr. Briar about it, and that made her suspicious. She was probably listening when we were talking about going to the folly. Remember there was that noise outside our door? It could have been her."

"Or Sam," added Sienna.

"You definitely don't have anything to feel bad about, Evie," said Ivy, smiling at her. "If it hadn't been for you, we'd never have found the secret button at the folly."

"Or the one that opened the staircase to the hidden room," said Lyra.

"I only found those buttons by falling over," said Evie.

"It's a very special talent, Evie," Sienna said.

"I'd call it unique," Lyra joined in with a grin.

"Definitely!" chuckled Ivy.

Evie saw the warmth in her friends' eyes, and

the knot of anxiety in her chest loosened. For the first time she started to believe that the rest of her dorm really didn't care that she was always having accidents and that maybe they did like her just the way she was.

"You're so smart, Evie," Ivy said, yawning as she turned off the light. "We wouldn't know nearly as much as we do now if we didn't have you."

I wish Sunshine felt the same, Evie thought as she snuggled down in bed. Sunshine had been fine with her when they'd been riding out to the tower, but she'd been quiet on the way home. When they got back, she'd seemed happy for Evie to leave her. Evie remembered all the times in the last week when Sunshine had wanted her to go away. *I wish she liked me more,* she thought, *but I bet she wishes she had another partner.*

She comforted herself by remembering what

her friends had just said. *I love being in Ruby dorm,* thought Evie happily, and with a smile she fell asleep.

★

At midnight the girls got out of their beds, dressed, and crept down the stairs. Evie was glad for her warm coat as she stepped outside. The night was chilly. Creatures rustled and squeaked from the bushes, and somewhere nearby, an owl hooted. Evie glanced back and saw a shadow move behind one of the upper windows where the staff bedrooms were. Her heart leaped into her throat. Was someone there, watching them? But no. When she looked again, the shadows behind the window were still.

"Come on!" Ivy grabbed her hand, and they ran silently across the dew-soaked grass to the stables. Ivy's grip tightened on Evie's hand whenever Evie tripped on a clump of grass.

Entering the stables, Evie's cheeks tingled with the sudden warmth. She went quickly to Sunshine's stall, walking softly so as not to disturb the other unicorns, snoring in their sleep.

Sunshine was awake, her dark eyes full of anxiety.

"We're still going, then?" she asked Evie.

"Yes." Evie sensed her unicorn's reluctance. "Why? Don't you want to?"

Sunshine looked awkward. "I do. It's just . . ." She trailed off.

Evie braced herself, sure that Sunshine was worried she was going to embarrass them in some way tonight. "What is it, Sunshine? Please tell me what's bothering you."

Sunshine glanced at her through her eyelashes. "I'm . . . I'm scared of the dark, Evie!"

Evie blinked. Of all the things she had been expecting Sunshine to say, it wasn't that. Hiding her surprise, she stroked Sunshine's cheek. "Really?"

"I always have been." Sunshine shuddered. "The grove was bad enough during the day; it's going to be even more scary at night."

"But Lyra has a flashlight, so we'll have light," said Evie gently. "And we'll all be together. Nothing will happen to you." As she comforted her, she felt a rush of relief. So this was why Sunshine had been quiet on the way home. It wasn't because she had been worried about Evie embarrassing her. It was because she'd been feeling scared about going back in the dark. "I'm really glad you told me," she said softly as Sunshine nuzzled her hands.

"Thanks for not laughing at me, Evie," Sunshine said gratefully. "I didn't want to say anything because I was worried that you'd think I was silly."

"I'd never think that," said Evie, stroking her.

Sunshine blew softly at Evie's face. "I'm so happy that you're my partner, Evie. Look, there's something I need to tell you—"

"Are you two ready?" interrupted Lyra, looking into Sunshine's stall. "We don't have much time," she added.

Evie sent Sunshine an apologetic look. "Tell me later," she whispered.

They followed the others outside and set off at a gallop.

★

When they reached Spiny Grove, they stopped. A bat swooped past as Lyra shone her powerful flashlight down the path.

Sienna gulped. "What if we see that ghost thing again?"

"It wasn't a ghost," said Lyra firmly.

"So what was it? It sounded spooky. *Whooooo*," said Sienna, mimicking the sound.

"I don't know what it was, but I promise you it wasn't a ghost," said Lyra, and she rode Misty into the trees.

Evie felt Sunshine hesitate and stroked her neck. "Don't be scared," she whispered. "Just focus on the light from the flashlight."

Sunshine nuzzled her leg before trotting after the others. To Evie's relief they reached the clearing with no ghostly encounters.

When they got there, they saw that Dr. Briar had secured the tower's wooden door with a new lock.

"Hopefully we won't need to use the door," said Lyra. "Where's that button, Evie? Let's press it and see what happens."

Evie slipped off Sunshine and crouched by the bench. Her fingers found the round button underneath it. "Here it goes!" She pushed it in.

There was a creaking, rumbling sound and part of the outer wall of the tower moved slowly back.

"Oh wow! There's a secret space between the

tower's inner and outer walls," said Lyra, jumping off Misty and going over to explore.

"A cavity!" exclaimed Sienna. "Just like the riddle said."

The space inside was totally dark. Evie felt very impressed as she peered inside. Ms. Evergreen must have been a gifted engineer to have constructed such a thing.

"I'm going in," said Lyra excitedly. They all followed—unicorns too. "Everyone look for the map!"

Evie's eyes followed the beam of the flashlight as Lyra shone it around. The cavity ran all around the outside of the tower. High above them was a window with no glass. It had a wide window ledge and there was something on it, but it was impossible to see what it was in the darkness. "Lyra, shine your flashlight up there," she said.

Lyra did so, and Evie saw a large nest of twigs.

Four owlets with fluffy gray baby feathers that glowed in the moonlight peered over the top, their large round eyes glowing in the flashlight beam.

Just then there was a hooting noise, and the mother owl flew in through the window, the feathers on her silvery wings shimmering. She landed on the nest and peered down curiously at the girls.

"WHOOOO-OOOO!"

Evie burst out laughing. "I think we've just found our ghost!"

"It was a specter owl!" said Ivy, her face a picture of relief. "They glow in the moonlight."

Sienna heaved a sigh. "Phew!"

"I wonder if Ms. Evergreen encouraged specter owls to nest here all those years ago," said Evie. "To make people think the folly was haunted."

Lyra swept her flashlight away from the nest so

as not to disturb the owls, and they continued to explore around the wall.

They were about halfway around the tower when Ivy cried out, "Stop, Lyra! There's something here."

Lyra shone the flashlight up the wall, revealing a small space carved into the stone above them. Lyra scrambled onto Misty and stood up on her back. She reached into the space and gasped. "There's something here! I can feel it!"

She pulled out some folded paper. Her eyes were huge in the flashlight as she sat down on Misty's back and held it out for everyone to see. It was old and yellow with spots of brown. Lyra's breath caught in her throat as she opened it up. "It's the third piece of the map!"

She turned it over, and they saw four lines of writing on the back.

"Another clue!" Evie exclaimed.

"If we solve it, we'll get the final piece!" said Ivy in excitement.

"And then we can find the Unicorn's Diamond!" cried Sienna.

A scraping noise echoed throughout the tower. Lyra's head snapped up. "What's that?"

The walls were moving! They groaned as they scraped across the ground to close up the gap.

"The entrance is shutting again! Everyone, move!" Lyra yelled.

They turned and raced back to where they had come in, but they were too late. With a deafening crash, the two walls met and the entrance disappeared. Evie's heart pounded against her ribs. They were trapped!

CHAPTER 9

"What happened?" cried Sienna, banging on the crack between the walls where the entrance had been.

"Why did the walls just shut like that?" said Ivy, her eyes scared.

"Listen!" Lyra motioned for everyone to stop talking.

Muffled voices came from the other side of the walls. It sounded like two people arguing.

"There's someone out there," said Sienna, frowning.

"Let us out!" shouted Lyra, thumping on the stone. The others joined in.

A sheet of paper slid through the crack between the two walls. Evie grabbed it. The paper was folded in half. Her fingers shook as she opened it and read aloud:

"HAND OVER THE MAP PIECES. IN RETURN, YOU WILL BE SET FREE. NO MAP, NO ESCAPE."

The girls stared at each other.

"Someone's locked us in here on purpose!" said Ivy.

"It has to be Dr. Briar," said Lyra.

"She can't have the map. Not when we're so close to finding the treasure," said Sienna.

Evie bit her lip. "We don't have a choice. Unless we hand it over, we could be trapped here forever."

Lyra's flashlight flickered. "The batteries are running out." She shook the flashlight in alarm.

"You mean we're going to be trapped in the dark?" Sunshine cried.

"It's okay, Sunshine," said Evie soothingly. "Just stay calm."

"I can't!" Sunshine's voice rose in panic as the flashlight beam flickered again. "No!" she whinnied, stamping her front hooves. Sparks flew up

and hit the wall. The stone shattered, and the girls shrieked as their unicorns dodged the flying pieces.

Lyra gasped. "What just happened?"

"It was Sunshine!" Ivy said, her eyes wide.

"Sunshine, you've just found your magic!" exclaimed Evie. "You have exploding magic!"

To Evie's surprise, Sunshine hung her head. "Actually I . . . I haven't just found it. I discovered it a few days ago. All the explosions that have been happening are my fault. Whenever I feel anxious and stamp my hooves, things just explode around me."

Evie stared at her. "Why didn't you tell me?"

Sunshine swallowed. "I didn't think you'd be very happy about me having exploding magic."

"Oh, Sunshine," said Evie, hugging her. "Of course I'm happy. Exploding magic is cool." A thought struck her. "Is this why you've been

asking me to leave you alone all week? You didn't want me to find out?"

Sunshine nodded. "I can't control it, and I thought you'd find that really embarrassing. It's awful. I could have really hurt us when the unicorn statue exploded."

"So that was you, not Dr. Briar or Sam?" Sienna said.

"Yes," muttered Sunshine.

"You should have told me. I could have helped you," said Evie. She hugged her unicorn tightly. "I thought that you wanted a different partner. I'm so embarrassing. It's true," she added when Sunshine started to shake her head. "I'm always having accidents. I know that's why you try to stop me from doing things."

"It's not that," said Sunshine in surprise. "I only want to stop you from getting hurt." She nuzzled

Evie. "But what about you? Are you okay with me having exploding magic? You don't like being the center of attention, and my magic is pretty hard to ignore."

Evie grinned. "I'm accident-prone and that's very tricky to hide! Sunshine, your magic makes you different and special, and I'd love you no matter what magic you had."

"Really?" asked Sunshine hopefully.

"Really," said Evie firmly.

Sunshine buried her head in Evie's arms, and Evie hugged her.

"Your hair, Evie!" gasped Ivy. She reached out and held up a strand of Evie's brown hair that had turned pink, turquoise, and yellow. "You've bonded!"

Evie felt a rush of delight. "We're partners forever, Sunshine!"

"Partners and best friends," said Sunshine happily.

"Now let's use your awesome magic to help us get out of here," said Evie. "Can you make a hole in the wall so we can escape?"

"I'll try," Sunshine said, tossing her mane. "Stand back, everyone, and watch out for flying stones."

Lyra put the new piece of the map in her pocket with the original pieces. Everyone shuffled back down the passageway, leaving Evie alone with Sunshine by the closed-up entrance.

"What if I explode the whole tower and hurt everyone?" asked Sunshine.

"You won't." Evie felt confident. "I know you're going to get your magic exactly right because you're the best, Sunshine!"

Sunshine took a deep breath and stamped her front hooves down hard. Bright pink sparks shot

up in the darkness. There was a strong smell of burnt sugar and, as the sparks hit the stone wall, a deafening bang. The stones exploded outward in a cloud of dust, making everyone cough. Through the swirling dust, Evie saw Flash and Solomon, Dr. Briar's unicorn, rearing backward in surprise. Dr. Briar and Sam clung to their unicorns' manes. The explosion seemed to have caught them in the middle of an argument.

"You're not going to get away with this!" Dr. Briar shouted. "Give me the map!"

"No way!" yelled Lyra, galloping out on Misty. "Ruby dorm, back to the academy, NOW!"

CHAPTER 10

Evie and Sunshine raced after their friends. "Are you okay?" Evie asked Sunshine. Magic was tiring for a unicorn when they first discovered their powers.

"I'm fine," said Sunshine. "I've already had quite a bit of practice at blowing things up!"

Evie hung on tightly to Sunshine's mane as they weaved through the trees. She could hear hooves pounding behind them. Glancing back, she saw Dr. Briar coming up fast on Solomon with Sam and Flash a short way behind.

"Hurry, Sunshine!" Evie yelled.

Solomon reached Sunshine and pushed alongside her. Dr. Briar leaned out to grab Evie's arm. "Give me the map!" she shrieked.

There was a sudden flash and a flurry of blue sparkles. Dr. Briar's hand froze, and Solomon stopped as if suspended in time. Evie's and Sam's eyes met for a second. He nodded, as if urging her on.

"Go!" yelled Evie to Sunshine.

Sunshine's hooves thundered loudly as she galloped out of the trees. At the edge of the woods, Evie glanced back. There was no sign of Dr. Briar or Sam, but she'd caught up with Misty, Sparkle, and Flame. By the time they arrived back at the stables, all four unicorns were dripping with sweat, their sides heaving.

Evie's legs were like jelly as she slid from Sunshine and threw her arms around her neck. "I thought Dr. Briar was going to grab me back in the woods."

"I can't believe Sam!" Sienna's eyes blazed. "He must have been working with his aunt all along. He's a total snake!"

"No, he's not!" Evie protested. "He helped me escape just now." She told the others what had happened. "If Flash hadn't frozen time, Dr. Briar would have pulled me off Sunshine."

Lyra frowned. "When we escaped, it looked like Sam and Dr. Briar were arguing. Maybe he was trying to stop her."

"Hmm," Sienna said, not looking convinced. "I still think he's a snake."

"Well, whoever's side he's on, the important thing is that we all got back safely," said Ivy.

"Should we tell the teachers what happened?" Evie asked.

"We'd get into really big trouble for sneaking out at night," said Sienna.

"And they'd make us hand over the map, and then we wouldn't be able to find the treasure," said Lyra.

"Let's not tell!" they all said together.

They grinned at each other.

"So this stays our secret," said Lyra.

Evie nodded. "We'd better watch out for Dr.

Briar, though. She's not going to give up that easily. Hopefully, she won't try anything here at school. Not with the teachers so close by."

"We'll have to be extra careful," Lyra said. "This next clue will lead us to the final piece of the map, and then we can find the treasure!" She patted her pocket. "I'm not going to let any of the pieces out of my sight."

The girls hurried into the stables and fetched their unicorns buckets of sky berries. Evie tipped the berries into Sunshine's manger, then kissed her on the muzzle. "Goodnight, Sunshine. See you tomorrow."

"Night, Evie." Sunshine blew her a kiss back, her dark eyes shining happily.

Evie's heart filled with joy. She was so glad she and Sunshine had sorted everything out. Now that she had found her magic and they had

bonded, they would definitely be graduating at the end of the year and be together forever.

"You know, I could stay here in the stables with you tonight," said Evie, not wanting to leave.

"You mean have a sleepover?" said Sunshine in delight.

Lyra poked her head into Sunshine's stall. "A sleepover in the stables! That's a wonderful idea! We could all squeeze in here together."

"But what about Dr. Briar?" said Evie, frowning. "She might try to attack us."

"Not with all the teachers' unicorns here," Lyra reassured her. "They'd raise the alarm in no time. I bet she won't try anything now we're back at school." She called to Ivy and Sienna. "What do you think about having a sleepover here tonight?"

The others agreed it was a great idea. While Ivy and Sienna got some warm rugs from the tack room, Lyra and Evie got some more straw and made Sunshine's bed super thick. Then they all squeezed inside. The unicorns laid down in the straw and the girls curled up next to them, covering themselves with the rugs and their unicorns' manes.

"Night, everyone," said Sienna, yawning.

One by one they fell asleep. Evie leaned her head against Sunshine's neck and closed her eyes.

Her heart swelled with happiness. She had the best friends in the world, a wonderful unicorn who loved her, and another adventure waiting just around the corner.

"I'm so glad you're my partner, Evie," Sunshine murmured.

Evie smiled and snuggled closer. "And I'm so glad you're mine!"

There's only one piece of the treasure map left to find! Can Ivy help Flame master his magic and solve the riddle?

Read on for a peek at the next book in the Unicorn Academy Treasure Hunt series!

"Look, Flame. A three-antlered deer! Isn't it cute?"

Ivy crouched down on her picnic blanket so as not to disturb the little creature that was grazing nearby. She munched her chocolate chip cookie and watched the deer.

"Mmm," said Flame. He tossed his head, and the sun lit up his golden mane, making its pink-and-green streaks sparkle.

Ivy gave Flame a curious look. "Are you okay? You've barely touched the picnic." She looked at all the food she'd brought—cheesy rolls, grapes, and chocolate chip cookies for herself, and apples, sky berries, and special unicorn cookies for Flame— and frowned. She had hoped the picnic would help them to bond. At home she loved having family picnics and sit-down meals with her brothers, sisters, and cousins, but Flame seemed distracted.

"Don't you like that?" she asked, looking at the cookie on the grass that he had only nibbled.

Flame sighed. "I do, but I'm not really in the mood for a picnic. Don't you think we should be trying to find my magic instead of sitting around?"

Ivy put her own cookie down and went over and hugged him. "Oh, Flame, don't worry. There's plenty of time for you to find your magic. Autumn's barely started, and we don't graduate until December."

"But I really want to discover my powers," said Flame impatiently. "Misty and Sunshine say it's so much fun doing magic."

Misty and Sunshine were paired with two of Ivy's roommates, Lyra and Evie. Misty had bubble magic, and Sunshine had exploding magic. Lyra and Evie also had flashes of color in their hair to match their unicorns' manes, which showed they had bonded with their unicorns. Bonding was the highest form of friendship. Students and unicorns were paired up when they arrived at Unicorn Academy. Once they discovered the unicorn's magical power and bonded, they could graduate and become guardians of the beautiful Unicorn Island.

Flame stamped a hoof. "There must be something we can do to help me find my powers."

Ivy stroked him. "Chill, Flame. I know it will be amazing to do magic, but just being at Unicorn Academy is tons of fun. So far it's been the best year of my life! Be patient and let it happen."

"What if it doesn't? What if we can't graduate and have to come back next year?" asked Flame.

Ivy kissed his nose. "Then we'll come back. Anyway, Sienna and Sparkle haven't discovered Sparkle's magic yet either, so it's not just us. Stop being such a worrywart."

In the distance, Ivy heard Lyra's voice, then Sienna's and Evie's joining in. She sighed. Lyra, Sienna, and Evie were her best friends, but they always wanted to do stuff instead of just hanging out and chatting. She bet they were looking for her now so they could make plans to search for the treasure map.

Back in January the four girls had discovered part of a treasure map hidden in a secret room in the school. They'd solved the riddle that was written on the back and found a second piece of the map behind an underground waterfall. The next riddle had led them to an old tower on the school grounds where they'd found the third quarter of the map. Now they just had to find the final piece so the map could show them how to reach the treasure, the legendary Unicorn's Diamond, a precious jewel that could grant people their heart's desire.

"Aren't you going to answer them?" asked Flame.

"I will," said Ivy, "but I'd really rather stay here. I wish I'd brought more food, then we all could have had a picnic together."

Flame plucked a long feathery strand of grass from the meadow and tickled Ivy's nose with it. "I like having adventures. Maybe one of them has solved the final riddle, and we can go on another scary quest!"

New friends. New adventures.
Find a new series ... just for you!

ISADORA MOON

For ballerina and fairy and vampire lovers

MAGIC ON THE MAP

For adventurers

UNICORN ACADEMY

For unicorn lovers

PUPPY PIRATES

For dog lovers

PURRMAIDS

For mermaid and cat lovers

BALLPARK Mysteries

For sports fans

RHCB rhcbooks.com

Collect all the books in the Horse Diaries series!